DAVY CROCKETT

Diana Herweck

Assistant Editor
Leslie Huber, M.A.

Editorial Director
Dona Herweck Rice

Editor-in-Chief
Sharon Coan, M.S.Ed.

Editorial Manager
Gisela Lee, M.A.

Creative Director
Lee Aucoin

Illustration Manager/Designer
Timothy J. Bradley

Cover Art and Illustration
Chad Thompson

Publisher
Rachelle Cracchiolo, M.S.Ed.

Teacher Created Materials, Inc.
5301 Oceanus Drive
Huntington Beach, CA 92649
http://www.tcmpub.com
ISBN 978-1-4333-0996-0
©2010 Teacher Created Materials, Inc.
Printed in China
YiCai.032019.CA201901471

Davy Crockett

Story Summary

It is August 17, 1786. A comet blazes across the sky, and suddenly a baby appears. It is none other than the legendary mountain man, Davy Crockett. Davy grapples with bears and panthers. Soon enough, they become his friends. He wears a talking coonskin cap, a gift from his loving mother. And he carries a rifle he calls Old Betsy, a gift from his dear old dad.

Davy grows to be an amazing young man. He can charm a raccoon out of a tree just by grinning at it. And that very same grin can strip the bark right off a tree! But what will happen when the sun freezes one day and no one knows what to do? Can Davy save the day? Read the story and find out!

Tips for Performing Reader's Theater

Adapted from Aaron Shepard

- Don't let your script hide your face. If you can't see the audience, your script is too high.

- Look up often when you speak. Don't just look at your script.

- Talk slowly so the audience knows what you are saying.

- Talk loudly so everyone can hear you.

- Talk with feelings. If the character is sad, let your voice be sad. If the character is surprised, let your voice be surprised.

- Stand up straight. Keep your hands and feet still.

- Remember that even when you are not talking, you are still your character.

- Narrator, be sure to give the characters enough time for their lines.

Tips for Performing
Reader's Theater *(cont.)*

- If the audience laughs, wait for them to stop before you speak again.

- If someone in the audience talks, don't pay attention.

- If someone walks into the room, don't pay attention.

- If you make a mistake, pretend it was right.

- If you drop something, try to leave it where it is until the audience is looking somewhere else.

- If a reader forgets to read his or her part, see if you can read the part instead, make something up, or just skip over it. Don't whisper to the reader!

- If a reader falls down during the performance, pretend it didn't happen.

Davy Crockett

Characters

Davy Crockett	Coonskin Cap
Bear	Narrator 1
Panther	Narrator 2

Setting

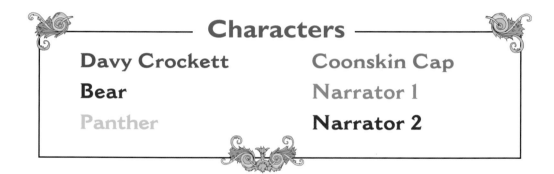

This reader's theater opens on a green mountaintop in Tennessee. The date is August 17, 1786, the day that Davy is born. The story ends on another Tennessee mountaintop, when Davy is a fully grown man.

Act I

Narrator 1: It was a warm day in the wild frontier. News had spread across the land that a comet was on its way. People were waiting for it to zoom through the sky. Night finally fell, and all eyes looked to the heavens. Out of nowhere, the comet came flashing past.

Narrator 2: It was like a great ball of fire. It zipped across the heavens and smashed right into the top of a Tennessee mountain. When the flash stopped, a baby boy fell to the earth, landing on his feet. It was Davy Crockett.

Narrator 1: And this is his story.

Davy Crockett: Wow! What just happened? I'm on a mountaintop in Tennessee, where the ground looks green and the land is free. I think I'm ready to see the world!

Narrator 2: Davy's parents found him there, and he went with them to his home in the woods. They placed him in his cradle made from a giant turtle shell.

Davy Crockett: And they fed me grizzly bear meat and gave me buffalo milk to drink. I grew so big and strong, I could whip my weight in wildcats!

Narrator 1: One day when Davy was three, he was eating his breakfast in the kitchen. Suddenly, a big grizzly bear walked in.

Bear: I'm feeling a bit hungry. I think I'll look in the cupboards and see what I can find to eat.

Narrator 2: And that bear started to open all the cupboards. He looked high, and he looked low. He looked on all the shelves until he found something promising.

Bear: Mmm, mmm! Yum! This jam looks delicious!

Narrator 1: And with that, he took the jar from the shelf and twisted the lid. He stuck his paw in the jar.

Bear: Oh, yum! Boysenberry jam is my favorite. I hope this is sweet!

Narrator 2: Right then, little Davy saw what the bear was doing. He did not want to share his food with the grizzly bear, and he was furious!

Davy Crockett: I'll teach you, Bear! I'm going to use my mighty arms to give you the biggest and strongest bear hug you ever got. It'll be a lesson you'll never forget!

Bear: But all I wanted was a sweet treat before I went on my way . . .

Davy Crockett: A gentleman always says "please"!

Narrator 1: With that, Davy jumped down from his chair and grabbed the bear. He wrapped his arms around the bear's big middle and hugged and hugged until that grizzly fell to the ground with a thud.

Davy Crockett: That'll teach you to mess with Davy Crockett! Some day, I'll be King of the Wild Frontier.

Narrator 2:   From that day on, everyone knew that Davy was a force to be reckoned with.

Bear: I'm sure not going to bother you again. Maybe I can be your friend. They say a man's best friend is his dog. How about a big old grizzly bear instead?

Davy Crockett: Well, I could use a friend.

Bear: Deal! Put her there, old pal!

Narrator 1:   Davy and the bear shook hands. Believe it or not, they became the best of friends. When Davy traveled around the frontier, Bear was sure to be at his side.

Act 2

Narrator 2: Years later, Davy's dad gave him his first rifle.

Davy Crockett: Living out in the woods, we needed a rifle to survive. There were a lot of pesky critters running around out there. Sometimes, we had to get them before they got us!

Bear: I thought that's what I was for! Don't I keep you safe? Can't I scare off the critters?

Davy Crockett: Oh, now, Bear! Let me tell my story without you interrupting. We'd shoot 'em with a rifle—I call mine Old Betsy—and then skin 'em for clothes and blankets.

Bear: Whew! I'm glad I'm your friend and not your blanket!

Narrator 1: Davy's mom also gave him something special. It was a coonskin cap.

Narrator 2: Every member of the Crockett family had one. It was a matter of pride to wear it. And it kept the head toasty warm.

Coonskin Cap: Why, thank you. I *am* a particularly cozy *chapeau*.

Narrator 1: One day, when Davy was out walking with Old Betsy and his coonskin cap, he came across a panther sitting in the middle of the forest.

Panther: Grrrowl! What's that boy up to?

Davy Crockett: I see something ahead in the forest. I think I'll have some fun.

Coonskin Cap: Be careful, Davy old boy.

Davy Crockett: Oh, now, just sit up there and hush, will you?

Narrator 2: Davy tiptoed closer.

Davy Crockett: Why, it's a panther! That old pussycat will never see me. I'll just flash Old Betsy and watch him run. He'll scamper like a little scaredy-cat.

Narrator 1: With that, Davy raised Old Betsy and . . .

Panther: Swat! I knocked that rifle right out of his hand.

Davy Crockett: I had to think fast. I grabbed the panther around his neck and started spinning. We went round and round. I knew he was getting dizzy.

Panther: I tried to shake him off, but no luck. So I scratched at him, raking him with my claws.

Narrator 2: The two rolled on the ground, thrashing back and forth and wrestling like there was no tomorrow.

Narrator 1: They each taught the other a big lesson.

Panther: I taught Davy to respect his wildlife brothers . . .

Davy Crockett: . . . and I taught Panther not to mess with
Davy Crockett.

Narrator 2:   But Davy never did try to scare another
panther after that day.

Act 3

Song: Home on the Range

Bear: One night when Davy and I were relaxing at
home, we heard a knock.

Narrator 1:   It was some of the townspeople, coming to see
if Davy wanted to go raccoon hunting.

Coonskin Cap: Well, Davy didn't like to hunt anything unless
he had a true need for it—like me.

Davy Crockett: I told them it was much too dark and
dangerous to go hunting.

Coonskin Cap: They should wait until daybreak.

Narrator 2: But they said it was a full moon and as bright as daylight.

Panther: Davy went outside to check it out.

Davy Crockett: Well, this is very strange. The full moon is not due for several days yet. What is making the sky shine so brightly?

Narrator 1: Davy knew it was not the moon.

Coonskin Cap: It was something else.

Davy Crockett: The sky sure is lit up, but that's no moon. That's a comet headed this way! If it crashes here, we'll have some big trouble. I've got to do something quick!

Narrator 2: No one knew what to do.

Narrator 1: The townspeople just stood by as Davy went running up to the top of a nearby mountain.

Bear: And I followed closely behind, just in case Davy needed me.

Coonskin Cap: And I stayed on his head, just for company.

Narrator 2: Davy stood on top of that mountain and reached his arms as high as he could. Up, up he stretched and . . .

Panther: . . . he grabbed the comet's tail! He swung around, whipping that comet along with him.

Narrator 1: Then he let go, flinging the comet right back from where it came.

Bear: Davy and I climbed back down the mountain, where the townspeople cheered. They told Davy he had done the impossible.

Coonskin Cap: But Davy knew it wasn't impossible. Nothing was impossible for Davy.

Davy Crockett: Just be sure you're right and then go ahead. You'll get the job done.

Act 4

Narrator 2: Years later, when he was running for political office, Davy boasted that he could grin a raccoon right out of a tree. That's right. He said that his powerful smile alone could charm that ring-tailed critter down to the ground.

Coonskin Cap: I sure seemed to be proof of it.

Panther: Well, someone decided to call him on his boast.

Bear: Late one night, Davy was awakened by the townspeople, wanting to see him get the raccoon out of the tree . . .

Panther: . . . just with his smile.

Bear: They challenged Davy to go into the forest then and there and work his charm.

Davy Crockett: I walked until I was deep in the dark forest. I came across a sprawling tree with a raccoon curled up high, and I started to smile. I gave that raccoon the broadest grin I'd ever grinned.

Coonskin Cap: Davy stood there with a wide grin across his face. The townspeople just watched.

Panther: But the more Davy stood there grinning, the more the raccoon just stayed curled up in a ball at the top of the tree.

Narrator 1: Davy grinned and grinned. But after quite a while and no raccoon, Davy got angry. He stormed out of the forest . . .

Bear: . . . and he returned with his axe.

Davy Crockett: I chopped and chopped with my handy axe, using all my strength until finally that tree came crashing down.

Narrator 2: It was then that Davy realized there was no raccoon!

Davy Crockett: Well, durn it. It was just a knothole in the tree! But looky here! I might not have grinned a raccoon down, but I did grin the bark right off the tree!

Coonskin Cap: It was true. That part of the tree was as smooth as can be.

Panther: The crowd cheered . . .

Bear: . . . and Davy won the election.

Act 5

Panther: Now get ready for an amazing story.

Narrator 1: One morning in the dead of winter, it was so cold that even the sun froze. Everyone was worried, but Davy knew just what to do.

Coonskin Cap: With me on his head and Bear on his back, he traveled to the peak of Daybreak Hill to see what he could do.

Davy Crockett: Well, looky here. Isn't this a mystery? What could be causing such a problem?

Narrator 2:   Davy examined what he found. He saw that the Earth had frozen, and the sun was jammed between the layers of ice.

Bear: He spit into each of his hands. Ptooey! Ptooey!

Coonskin Cap: Then, he rubbed his hands together to get them nice and warm.

Bear: Then, with a heave and a ho, he just wrenched that sun free!

Coonskin Cap: And everything was right as rain.

Davy Crockett: I went back down the hill whistling, with a piece of the sunrise in my pocket.

Bear: People thought Davy should have been scared on that chilly day.

Panther: But as Davy always says . . .

Davy Crockett: Be sure you're right, then go ahead.

Poem: Farewell to the Mountains

Narrator 1:   Now that you've heard Davy's story, you know a thing or two about him.

Narrator 2:   But keep in mind that we may have stretched the truth, just a bit.

Narrator 1:   Davy Crockett was a real man, and he did some important things.

Narrator 2:   Folks who know the story of the Alamo know that he was a true American hero. And that's no tall tale!

Farewell to the Mountains

by David Crockett

Farewell to the mountains whose mazes to me
Were more beautiful far than Eden could be;
No fruit was forbidden, but Nature had spread
Her bountiful board, and her children were fed.
The hills were our garners—our herds wildly grew,
And Nature was shepherd and husbandman too.
I felt like a monarch, yet thought like a man,
As I thanked the Great Giver, and worshipped his plan.

Home on the Range

original version by
Brewster Higley and Daniel Kelley

Oh, give me a home where the buffalo roam,
Where the deer and the antelope play,
Where seldom is heard a discouraging word,
And the skies are not cloudy all day.

Chorus:
Home, home on the range,
Where the deer and the antelope play,
Where seldom is heard a discouraging word,
And the skies are not cloudy all day.

How often at night when the heavens are bright
With the light from the glittering stars,
Have I stood there amazed and asked as I gazed
If their glory exceeds that of ours.

Chorus

Where the air is so pure, the zephyrs so free,
The breezes so balmy and light,
That I would not exchange my home on the range
For all the cities so bright.

Chorus

Glossary

balmy — mild; soothing

bountiful — abundant; plentiful

chapeau — the French word for *hat*

comet — an object in space that orbits the sun, with a center of dust and gas that trails behind it like a tail

coonskin cap — a hat made from the fur of a raccoon

discouraging — disheartening; opposing

exceeds — goes beyond

garners — buildings for storing grain

husbandman — farmer

knothole — a hole in a tree or board

monarch — a king or queen

political — having to do with running a government

promising — full of hope and possibilities

raking — scratching with claws or tines

sprawling — spreading or reaching out in all directions

zephyrs — gentle breezes